A NOTE ABOUT THE STORY

Donald Charles is technically not the anthropologist in his family; that distinction belongs to his brother, Dr. Clement W. Meighan. But Mr. Charles has always been fascinated with the stories and artwork of other cultures, and has amassed an extensive collection of images from ethnic Peruvian art.

The inspiration for *Chancay and the Secret of Fire* came from an ancient Peruvian tapestry showing a mysterious winged figure holding a torch. The figure began to take on a life of its own, and eventually a name: Chancay, derived from that of a long-vanished pre-Columbian tribe.

But Chancay, the character, thrived in Donald Charles's imagination. Following a hallowed folkloric tradition, the author fit the figure on the tapestry to an imagined explanation of natural phenomena: the appearance of the moon, and the relationship of the sun to fire on the earth. Culling images and patterns from the carvings, paintings, metalwork, ceramics, and textiles of pre-Columbian Peru, the artist's exciting recreation of the folk art from that culture is beautifully adapted to the picture book form. Mr. Charles bridges a gap of centuries and cultures to bring the stylized figure of Chancay to life as a brave, kind man bringing fire to his people and light to our imaginations.

Tomie dePaola, Creative Director
WHITEBIRD BOOKS

CHANCAY AND THE SECRET OF FIRE

A Peruvian folktale written and illustrated by

DONALD CHARLES

A WHITEBIRD BOOK
G. P. Putnam's Sons
New York

IN MEMORY OF HEITOR VILLA-LOBOS
—D. C.

Text and illustrations copyright © 1992 by Donald Charles
All rights reserved. This book, or parts thereof, may not be reproduced
in any form without permission in writing from the publisher.
G. P. Putnam's Sons, a division of The Putnam & Grosset Group,
200 Madison Avenue, New York, NY 10016. Published simultaneously in Canada.
Printed in Hong Kong by South China Printing Co. (1988) Ltd.
Book design by Gunta Alexander.   The text is set in Weiss.
Library of Congress Cataloging-in-Publication Data
Charles, Donald.   Chancay and the secret of fire: a Peruvian folktale
/ written and illustrated by Donald Charles.   p.   cm.   "A Whitebird book."
Summary: As a reward for releasing the beautiful fish he has caught, Chancay is
granted his wish of finding a way to relieve his people from the cold and darkness.
[1. Fire—Fiction.] I. Title PZ7.C374Ch 1992 [E]—dc20 91-16629 CIP AC
ISBN 0-399-22129-8
1   3   5   7   9   10   8   6   4   2
First Impression

Many, many years ago, before the building of the great city of Chan Chan, or the hidden mountain temples; before the grand pyramids to the Sun and Moon, there lived a man called Chancay.

Early one morning, Chancay left his stone village in search of a new place to fish. He followed the sound of a waterfall, hidden in the mists, until he came to a silver pool nestled in dark, slippery boulders.

The instant Chancay cast his net into the icy waters,
he felt the heavy tug of a large, struggling creature.

Chancay strained with all his might, and pulled his net
to the surface. There, to his astonishment, was an
enormous fish of many brilliant colors.

The strangeness and beauty of the creature caught Chancay by surprise.

"This thing is far too beautiful to be killed and eaten," Chancay said aloud. "Even though I am hungry, I will let this fish go." And Chancay opened the net so the fish could escape.

Then the fish rose from the water, sat on a square rock, and spoke to Chancay. "I am Tambo, a Spirit of Father Earth. Because you have shown the kindness of your soul, I will give you one favor. Tell me what you would like."

"I seek nothing for myself," replied Chancay, when he had found his voice, "but my people suffer from the cold, and are afraid in the blackness of the night."

"You need the gift of fire," said Tambo, "to warm your stone houses, to cook your food, and to light your way when the sun sleeps beyond the sea."

"How can we find this fire?" asked Chancay.

Tambo said, "It is a secret to be learned, and a secret to be earned. Are you ready for such a task?"

"I am," said Chancay. "What must I do?"

"There will be a great storm tomorrow," Tambo replied. "You must climb to the highest peak and hold a basin laden with stones above your head."

Then he slipped from the rock and vanished beneath the waters.

The next day, Chancay labored to the top of the highest peak, carrying the heavy basin. Angry clouds gathered as thunder rumbled and echoed through the valleys.

Finally, Chancay stood, struggling to lift his burden against the cutting winds and freezing rains. "I have come from Tambo," he cried. "Please give me the secret of fire."

Just as he said these words, a great flash of lightning broke from the clouds and shattered the bowl in Chancay's hands. Wearily, he made his way down the mountain, battered and disappointed.

The next day Chancay went to the silver pool. "You have tricked me, Tambo!" he cried to the water. "I could not capture the lightning."

Tambo lifted his head from the pool. "I already know you are kind," he said, "but that will not be enough for the task you have before you. Now you have proved that you are also strong."

"Very well," said Chancay. "What must I do next?"

"Put your face to the south wind," Tambo said, "and walk four days. There you will find fire at your feet." And once again, Tambo vanished in rings of silver ripples.

So Chancay filled a sack with sweet potatoes to eat, wrapped a blanket of llama wool around his shoulders, and set off into the south wind.

The first day, Chancay crossed a valley of stinging spiders, but he wrapped his feet and legs in reeds to avoid being bitten.

The second day, Chancay found himself in a rocky
field of snakes, but he was able to fend them off with his
walking stick.

The third day, Chancay climbed through a mountain pass filled with crouching pumas. He swung his ax around his head and made it safely to the next valley. At night he huddled in a dark cave.

On the fourth day, Chancay came upon a smoldering crater in the ground. In the center of the crater, molten red rocks bubbled and hissed. At the edges, clouds of yellow steam drifted from the earth.

Chancay picked up warm rocks at the edge of the crater, but they soon cooled in his hands. He leaned toward the fiery rocks at the center, but the fierce heat drove him back.

"Tambo has sent me on another fool's errand," he told himself as he turned to retrace his dangerous journey.

When he reached his own village, he found a condor sitting on his windowsill.

"Tambo has sent me to lend you my wings," the condor said. "You have now proved yourself brave, as well as strong and kind. You are ready to take the secret of fire from the Kingdom of the Sun and Moon."

"Is this another trick?" demanded Chancay.

"Oh, no," replied the condor. "My wings will carry you to where the Sun and Moon dwell above the sky. The Moon has a golden mirror in which she admires herself. You must steal the mirror and bring it back to Tambo."

"What if I am caught by the Sun?" Chancay asked.

"Then you will be turned into a shower of sparks, and cast forever into the night. Each of the stars is a soul who has tried to steal the secret of fire."

Chancay took the condor's wings and flew higher and higher, beyond the clouds, above the sky, to a bright golden temple where the Sun and Moon lived.

In the great hall he hid behind a pillar and saw the Moon admiring her reflection in a shiny disk. He knew he must think of a clever plan if he would succeed where so many had failed.

Chancay knew that once a month the Moon did not appear in the sky, and he reasoned that on cloudy days, the Sun must also sleep.

So he waited patiently for many days and nights until, at last, the Sun and Moon were both asleep. Then he seized the golden mirror and flew to earth as swiftly as a falling stone.

Chancay flew straight to the silver pool and called for
Tambo. "How do I use the Moon's mirror?" he cried.

"When the Sun wakes, he will be very angry, and he
will seek you out with one of his powerful rays," said
Tambo. "You must catch his rays in the mirror and direct
them into a bundle of twigs and reeds."

And so Chancay did just as Tambo had told him, and
the bundle of twigs and reeds burst into flame.

Now the people were able to keep warm, and to light their way in the dark.

And ever since, the Sun continues to shine his searching rays on every corner of the land, and the Moon must be content admiring her reflection in lakes and rivers and the lonely sea.